THE FINAL VOW

CON'S WEDDING NOVELLA

Secrets and Lies Series

BJ Alpha

Cover by Katie Evans

Edited and Proofread by Dee Houpt

Proofread by Cheyenne Sampson

 Created with Vellum

Dedication

To everyone who has lived with mental health issues. I hope my writing brings you the same happiness it brings me.

AUTHORS NOTE

This book contains: violence, sexual graphic scenes and strong language. It is for ages eighteen and over.

This novella is connected to the Secrets and Lies Series.
Set after the Secrets and Lies Series has been completed.
If you haven't read the Secrets and Lies Series yet, you
can find them on Amazon and Kindle Unlimited.

<u>Secrets and Lies Series</u>

CAL Book 1

CON Book 2

FINN Book 3

BREN Book 4

OSCAR Book 5

THE FINAL VOW

BJ ALPHA

Chapter One

Will

After what feels like a lifetime, the day has finally arrived. Con and I have been through hell and back, but today . . .

Today, I will become Mrs. O'Connell.

Con, along with most of his family and all the children, have stayed over at the venue. Lily and Angel—his brothers' wives—and I stayed at a nearby hotel and are currently being driven in a limousine to the event to get ready.

The event I haven't even seen yet because my fiancé has taken the wedding planning on and has become so engrossed in it that after the mention of a zoo theme, I threw in the towel and told him to organize the damn thing himself.

Honestly, I couldn't care less where, when, or how we get married as long as our son, Keen, is with us on our big day.

But Con? He's an all-out groomzilla to the extreme, making sure this is the biggest, most extravagant, and most elaborate wedding ever to don the Mafia world.

"Will, are you okay? We're almost there," Lily, Cal's wife, asks from opposite me. My eyes snap to hers, not realizing I'd zoned out.

"I'm fine. A little anxious as to what's in store, but fine." I wince as I admit my nerves, not at being married, no, worried at what the hell he has planned.

Angel laughs. "You should be nervous. Finn told me he ordered a fucking tiger!"

I scrunch my nose. I know Con has big ambitions with the wedding, but a tiger is a little far-fetched. Surely, they're kidding. Right?

My mind darts back to our conversation about the zoo theme, and I grimace at the memory of Con suggesting we ride in on camels. I mean, camels? As though we live in the Middle East. What. The. Actual. Fuck?

When I suggested animal control might have something to say about it, Con burst out laughing and told me money talks; I rolled my eyes and told him I'd leave him at the altar if he organized a zoo wedding. No. Freaking. Way.

I glance out the window, and my mouth drops at the amazing view ahead.

Oh wow, it's absolutely beautiful, picture-perfect. Mountains are on either side of us, almost caving us in. The limo slows as we approach a security gate, and various security measures are taken, including scanning the undercarriage of the vehicle.

The limo begins the steady drive over the cobbled stones, and before long, an enormous building comes into view; it's a modern type of cabin with glass windows encompassing the entire frontage, giving way to the amazing views of the mountains.

"Holy shit, this is incredible." Angel gasps beside me.

"Oh wow, Will. The photos are going to be so good. Stunning." Lily's smile spreads over her face.

My smile mirrors hers, and excitement bubbles in my stomach.

Con

Everything that could go wrong has gone wrong. Even the damn tiger has been sick on the journey up here.

"Remind me again, why the fuck did you seat Lorrenzo Varros next to the Riccis?" Cal barks in my direction, pissing me off. He's pacing up and down the suite, stressing the hell out over seating plans. "This is a fucking disaster," he snaps at me and throws one of those laser glares at me too, making me roll my eyes.

I mean, it's my fucking wedding. I should be able to seat them wherever the hell I want. Besides, he had the floor plan weeks ago; why didn't he bring it up then?

"The girls have arrived," Oscar declares. My shoulders relax. She's here. She's actually fucking here.

A hand lands on my shoulder and tightens. "You good, brother?" Bren's gruff voice makes my eyes meet his.

I nod nervously. "Yeah, I'm good." Bren's lips tighten into a smile.

Since he got with his woman, Sky, the man has loosened up to no end, and now, I'd even consider him vaguely human.

Bren's eyebrows furrow as he stares over my shoulder. "Why the fuck is Keen pissing in the planter?"

I spin around, annoyed, to find my six-year-old son pissing into a plant pot. My mouth drops open; what the hell? "Keen? Why are you peeing in the planter, dude?"

Keen's cute face turns toward me, and my composure instantly relaxes at my son. "Uncle Finn said the bathroom is busy, so I had to use a bush."

I turn and glare at Finn. He's sitting with his feet up on the coffee table and a toothpick hanging from his lip, a huge grin encompassing his cocky face.

My jaw ticks in frustration. He's so fucking nonchalant when it comes to parenting; it pisses me the hell off.

Finn shrugs. "Prince is on the toilet; the kid has to piss somewhere. I mean, I meant outside, but clearly, the poor kid takes after you for lack of common sense."

I sneer at him, my temples pulsating. "You fucking jackass. He's six."

Finn shrugs again. "Pretty sure it wouldn't make a difference if he was thirty-six; the kid is your fucking double."

I'm sure Finn is trying to insult me, but honestly? I'm beaming with fucking pride, knowing Keen is like me. A mini-Con.

"He's been in there a while, man; you sure he's okay?" Bren asks while staring at the bathroom door, his face etched in concern.

Finn waves his hand in the bathroom's direction. "He's fucking fine. He has his tablet and snacks. I won't lose him in the little toilet seat thing."

"He's a little young to be on the toilet. Isn't he?" Oscar asks with uncertainty.

"Fuck if I know. Angel said we could have another kid when he's potty trained, so . . . I Googled and got him a seat. Kid will be trained in no time." He shrugs.

I mean, I wasn't around when Keen was toilet-trained, but I'm pretty damn sure it isn't as easy as Finn thinks.

"You put Kozlov on the opposite side of the hotel, right?" Cal asks, still pacing.

My eyes narrow; did he not read the plans at all? Just what the hell does he do for this family?

"Security is established. Calm the hell down," Oscar finally snaps, saving me from doing it.

"I sure as shit don't take after you," Reece throws in without lifting his head from his tablet. Cal follows the insult up with a glare in Reece's direction.

Bren exhales loudly. "I'm gonna go check on Sky and the kids."

"Yeah, sure you are." Finn smirks.

Chapter Two

Bren

I swipe the door with my key card and smile at the scene before me as I enter. Sky has Charlie and Chloe, my nieces, playing with dolls on the floor, while our son, Seb, sits munching on Cheerios, watching some crazy cartoon pig Keen has him hooked on. Little Samuel is asleep in his fold-away crib beside the couch.

My heart swells at the sight of my family.

I need to give my woman a little girl, and then we'll be complete.

"Bren, I didn't expect you back." Sky stands and walks toward me; my heart hammers in my chest like all the other times my girl greets me.

I push my hand through her long blonde hair and tug her by the neck toward me. "Missed you, baby." I nuzzle into her, making her break out in a shiver and giggles that makes my cock swell in these tight-as-fuck penguin pants.

"You were with me only a couple of hours ago." She

pulls back and lifts an eyebrow; her blue eyes sparkle with fun, and she nibbles on her lip playfully.

I draw back into her smooth golden hair, smelling my scent on her. "Mmm, fucking need you already, Sky." I grind my solid cock into her hip for effect. Even after fucking her this morning, I still need more.

It's never enough. Never.

"Charlie, can you be a big girl and keep an eye on the little ones while I show Uncle Bren a leaky tap in the bathroom?"

Charlie's head spins in our direction. Her dark eyes meet mine, and the kid breaks out into a huge smile. "Sure."

I nod at my niece and follow Sky down the corridor into the bathroom.

As soon as the door closes, I'm on her, tugging up the cute little dress she has on. "Gonna have to be real quick, baby," I mumble with need.

"Yes. Please hurry." Sky pants as she clutches on to the bathroom countertop, her toned, bare ass on display for me. Fuck, she's incredible.

I make quick work of unbuckling my pants and freeing my cock from my boxers; pre-cum leaks from the end. I don't want any of it wasted; I swipe it up with my thumb and, using my free hand, I separate Sky's ass cheeks. Using my thumb, I ram into her tight hole, chuckling sadistically when she jolts at the intrusion. I twist my thumb around inside her ass while positioning my cock at her pussy entrance. Her cream is already dripping as I rub my cock up and down her hole, then plunge forward, forcing her to hit her hips on the counter.

"Oh god, Bren." Her head drops forward, and her hair acts like a curtain around her. I draw back and slam into her again, reveling in the feel of her dripping heat.

Fuck me, that's good.

I move my now free hand up to her long blonde locks and wrap it around my fist, tugging her head back so her neck is strained, and she winces at the force. Her gorgeous neck is pulled back tight, her sky-blue eyes locked on to mine in the mirror.

With the other hand firmly gripping her ass cheek and my thumb pressed in her puckered hole, I continuously pull back and slam into her.

"Fuck, baby. Open your buttons. I wanna see your tits bounce."

Sky fumbles to open the buttons to the top half of her dress, and the few buttons make it so she has to withdraw her tits through a small opening, forcing them together. The sight has my balls tingling; her nipples are almost kissing. She brings her hands up to her breasts and plays with her nipples, knowing how much it turns me on. Her pussy clenches on my cock, and I grit my teeth at the overloading sensation, trying to ward off my orgasm.

My eyes lock on to Sky's tits, now leaking milk for our babies.

Oh shit.

I withdraw and slam in. Sky's mouth falls open on a silent scream.

Holy fuck. I slam harder. Fuck. Those tits. Fuck.

Holy shit, I come hard.

"Fuuuuck," I grit through clenched teeth, trying not to disturb the kids.

My cock finally stops pumping, and I reluctantly withdraw from my girl. Cum runs down her thighs, and the asshole in me loves it.

My gorgeous girl's chest heaves up and down, her face flushed red with arousal.

"You good, baby?" I kiss her neck tenderly, over the tattoo marking my ownership of her.

"Mmm. Yes." She grins lazily like a satiated kitten.

"Good girl. Clean up and look after the babies. I'll see you later." I tuck my spent cock into my pants and give her one final nuzzle. "Forever," I mumble into her hair.

Sky smiles back at me while I wait for her to repeat the word. "Forever."

Will

I throw my arms around Sky; she traveled here with the men.

Apparently, it is because the kids were being kept together, and Sky is still breastfeeding her boys, Sebastian and Samuel, but we all know it's because Bren refuses to let her leave his side. He's a complete neanderthal and the worst of the O'Connell brothers for it.

"Are the guys okay?" I ask her as she bounces Samuel in one arm and struggles with Sebastian in the other.

"Oh, they're fine. Bren came by earlier." She blushes profusely, and I can't help but smile at her sweet innocence, oblivious to the fact she's giving away exactly what Bren came by for earlier.

When Sky was found trafficked in a crate that wasn't meant to be delivered to the family's warehouse, the guys discovered a whole human trafficking ring their uncle was once a part of. Sky was literally trained to be someone's submissive; she's come on in leaps and bounds while in our family, but the poor girl has been through so much. Luckily, Bren is amazing with her, but with that comes a fierce determination to protect her; therefore, he becomes overzealous and super protective.

"Mom, when do we get to dress up?" Charlie asks while bouncing up and down.

Finn and Angel's daughter is a bundle of energy at ten years old; she's a mother hen to all the younger kids, but this girl is wise beyond her years. She keeps both her parents on their toes while getting Finn to eat out the palm of her hand.

Angel throws herself down in the armchair. She looks exhausted. For the first time in a long while, I take notice of her. There are dark circles under her eyes, and she looks pale.

As if sensing me watching her, her eyes lock on to mine. There's panic in her bright-green eyes, and I furrow my eyebrows as I scan over her body, looking for something to explain her behavior and appearance . . .

The penthouse door swings open unexpectedly, and without warning, Reece walks into the room like he owns it.

"Jesus, Reece, we could have all been changing!" Lily snipes at her son.

He's eighteen years old and looks like a fully grown man; I have to shake myself at how quickly my nephew has grown up.

Reece scrunches his nose in utter disgust. "Why the fu—" He doesn't get to finish the sentence because Lily throws her hand over his mouth to stop him.

"Did you want something, Reece?" I ask, grinning at my nephew.

Lily releases his mouth. "Yeah, Con said to tell you to start getting ready." We all look at one another in confusion because did he really come in here to state the obvious? "Oh, and the hairdresser can't make it."

My shoulders tighten, panic builds inside me, and my mouth drops open. "What?"

"You could have started with that, Reece." Lily exhales in frustration.

He waves a hand at her as though swatting a fly. "Con's flying someone in. They'll be here in time."

My shoulders sag in relief.

"Oh, and I have to give you this." He hands me a small envelope, then turns and leaves the room a hell of a lot quieter than when he arrived.

I open the small black envelope and take out the note in Con's messy handwriting. I read his words:

Broken beyond repair, I needed you to show me that you care. Fractured into a thousand pieces, filled with self-loathing. Safe in your arms around me. You saved me from myself.

My eyes fill with tears as I choke on a sob.

When Con tracked me down to find me living with our son, he refused to give up on us, determined to make us a family. We had hurdles to climb, including Con having to work through depression and PTSD, but we're finally here.

Where we should have always been.

Chapter Three

Con

I tighten the bow tie around my neck and step back to get a better view of myself. Fuck, I look good. It's been a long road to being able to be proud of the man staring back at me in the mirror, but I stand taller with the confidence I've grown.

Not just in myself, but in my relationship with Will, too.

Since getting back together, it's been a constant internal struggle that I worry I'm not good enough for her, that she'll realize it someday and leave me. But with the help of therapists and Will, I've come to acknowledge the fact that she loves me just the way I am.

She loves me.

"Proud of you, little brother." Bren stands behind me with a smirk.

"Yeah, you scrub up okay, ya little shit." Finn grins while adjusting his messy hair.

"We're all proud of you." Cal nods at me as he lines up with my brothers, all standing behind me, towers of support.

I choke on emotion as I take in their reflections, always behind me.

Always there.

Oscar sidles into the mirror as well and fidgets uncomfortably, adjusting his jacket sleeves. "We're going to be late." His lip curls into a smirk, and I grin back at him, knowing he's proud of me, too.

I slap my brother on the back then wince at his jolt, forgetting in the moment that Oscar doesn't like any physical contact. His step falters before he straightens his shoulders as though trying not to make too big of a deal out of his reaction toward me.

"Jesus, what the fuck is that smell?" Finn scowls, breaking the awkward moment.

"Peppa did a poopy," Keen declares while rocking back and forth on his heels with a cheeky grin.

My face drops into shock. "Where?"

Keen throws his arm out. "Everywhere."

We scan the carpet, and sure as shit, my Chinese-crested baby has the shits. Again. "He suffers with nerves," I tell my brothers with a shrug before they all diss my dog.

Cal

The room fills with guests, and trepidation flows in my veins.

Every important close family member of each Mafia don fills the room. Kozlov takes a seat toward the back. His broad shoulders and scarred face scream both power and corruption. His right-hand man, Dimitri, sits stoically still beside him. They're the only members of the Russian Bratva to be invited, and although we don't work alongside them, we have a good relationship with them. More out of necessity than anything else. We both work in firearms but maintain a dignified distance to ensure our businesses do not coincide. With that in mind and the recent contract Bren signed off on, it was to be expected that we'd invite them along today.

Reece comes to stand beside me, and my shoulders broaden in pride at my son. At eighteen, he has the world at his feet. Countless Ivy League universities are knocking on his door, desperate to enroll his amazing mind and talents in one of their specialist academies. He has high-functioning autism, something he's learned to use as an asset instead of a hindrance.

Reece has decided to take a year off after finishing school and grow his business in the entertainment industry. He plans to buy failing bars and clubs and turn them around with new innovative ideas. He has to be twenty-one to do that, so while he's waiting, he will be taking a business management course at the local university, something I'm not too happy about, but I must admit, I was relieved when I found out he will be staying home. I'm not quite ready for my son to move out, not after only finding him and my wife, Lily, a few years ago, and I sure as hell will not let him be taken advantage of.

I gaze down toward my ma, and she beams up at me; Oscar's woman, Paige, sits beside her. She chose to forgo being a bridesmaid to support Ma, something we were all grateful for.

Con and Finn practically swagger down the aisle with cocky smirks on their faces. Looking over at Bren standing beside me, he rolls his eyes at their antics, making me stifle a laugh.

Con steps onto the stage and chats with the officiant while I scan the room once again, my whole body on edge with nerves, both at the gravity of this event and knowing what I've arranged later. I need it to run without a hitch. Worrying about them both running smoothly, I drag a hand through my hair in agitation.

Diverting my attention and trying to relax, I turn and take in the amazing view from behind the stage.

Full-length glass windows give way to an open view of the lake in front of us.

Now being dusk, Con had insisted on the wedding starting later than normal for the sun to set as they tie the knot. Pretty sure he stole that idea from Bren's wedding, but no one has dared to call him out on it.

A band set up in the corner of the room plays low music.

Candle-lit lanterns surround us, flickering off the mirrored floor that has been laid down as an aisle.

Deep-red roses are tied on the back of each chair, giving it an elegant, romantic feel.

My gaze flits over the crowd and unwillingly latches on to Luca Varros. Since his sister was brutally murdered by a member of the Ricci Family, Luca has been out for blood. He's held such a vendetta against them that his Don, Lorrenzo, forced him to marry the Ricci Mafia Princess, Camille. The poor girl looks miserable and nervous as hell, but she's clearly trying her best to hide it.

As if sensing my gaze, Luca narrows his eyes in my direction; they are cold and scream violence. He's known to be ruthless, so much so, his own men were being slaughtered in his determination to wipe out the Ricci Family empire. Camille must have one hell of a life with him. I nod politely in his direction, but the cold prick just stares me down.

I shake my head in amusement and turn back toward the entrance when the music changes, and the room falls silent.

Chapter Four

Finn

I stand beside my little brother, watching him closely. Con has been through the depths of Hell, and I couldn't be prouder of how he has overcome all of his issues to be standing here today for the woman he loves.

The only woman he has ever loved.

I turn my back to the guests and pull my phone out, scanning the messages from Angel last night.

> FinnFitty: Send me a photo of your tits. I need some material to fuck my hand to.

> Angel: You got the real thing this morning.

> FinnFitty: Darlin', come on . . .

> Angel: You're having a family meal right now, right? I'm not sending you images of my tits while you sit next to your ma.

FinnFitty: Darlin', I'm sitting next to Bren, and he's finger fucking Sky under the damn table again.

Angel: Oh my god! He is not!

FinnFitty: Fuckin' swear it.

Angel: I'm sure you have plenty of photos of my tits already, Finn.

FinnFitty: Darlin', come on. I need fresh spank bank material. I need you to push them together and do that thing where your nipples touch.

FinnFitty: Swear to fuck, your nipples are getting bigger.

FinnFitty: Gets me so damn hard.

FinnFitty: Darlin' . . .

FinnFitty: Darlin', you fucking ignoring me now?

FinnFitty: ANGEL!!!

FinnFitty: FUCKIN' ANSWER ME!

FinnFitty: Ringing you.

My eyebrows furrow at my phone. When I called her, she was pissed, that's for sure. I think back over how I left the apartment yesterday. Pretty fuckin' sure I emptied the dishwasher like she told me to, so she can't have attitude over that. And I remembered all of Prince's shit from the list she left me. My jaw clenches in frustration. Her tone was off this morning, too. The sooner this wedding is over, the better; I need to make sure my woman is okay with me, and the thought that she isn't is making me angsty as hell.

I grind my teeth in frustration, already willing this damn performance to hurry the hell up and finish already.

The band changes the music, and everyone falls silent.

The lead singer, Jonah Baker, sings an acoustic version of "Anyone" by Justin Bieber.

The doors open at the rear of the room, and all eyes follow the sounds of the footsteps.

Sky walks down the aisle first with baby Samuel in her arms and Sebastian toddling beside her, both little guys in mini tuxedos to match our own.

Angel said all the women would wear off-the-shoulder dresses the same color as the flowers. At first, this pissed me off because I'd prefer Angel covered up. I don't need any of these fuckers checking her rack out, but she assured me the beauties would be tucked away, and she promised she'd give me a private show later. I mean, I know she's pissed at something, but she can't go back on a promise.

Sky goes straight to Bren, who looks like he's ready to rip her dress off her, his eyes heavy and devouring her every movement. The thought makes me subtly smirk in his direction.

Lily walks down next, her eyes latching on to Cal's, as though they're the only two people in the room.

My heart pumps faster, knowing it's Angel who will walk down the aisle next; the click of her heels against the mirrored floor makes me slowly drag my eyes up to my gorgeous woman. Her tattooed arms are exposed, and I couldn't be prouder of my wife showing the world who she is: a strong, independent fighter and, better still, an amazing mother to our kids, and she's my wife. Her angry eyes latch on to mine, making my eyebrows furrow.

Yeah, she's pissed.

I quickly glance around the room, looking for clues, before I settle back on her. Angel's expression softens the closer she gets, as though she can't stay pissed for long at whatever it is I've done.

As she gets within arm's reach of me, I snap my arm out, wrapping it around her waist, and tug her in for a chastising kiss.

When I draw back, I scan her face. "We good?" I query with a raised brow.

She clamps her jaw shut, as though she's struggling to find a reply to my question.

Shit, I've definitely done something.

Angel steps to stand beside me as we watch the movement down the aisle.

My heart soars when my gorgeous daughter, Princess, my mini-Angel, breezes down the aisle with confidence and a gracious smile encompassing her face.

She drops blood-red rose petals onto the floor, and I swallow the emotion of being a proud father.

"Where's Prince?" Angel whispers in my ear.

"Huh?" I turn my head slightly, wondering if I misheard her.

"Prince. Where the hell is Prince?"

I jolt at her words. Oh shit.

Panic floods me. Holy fucking shit. I spin on my heel, making Con glare at me. I try to subtly move past Bren, but the guy's a tank blocking the exit.

"Problem?" He side-eyes me with annoyance in his tone.

"Yeah, I, err"—I scrub a hand through my hair—"I forgot Prince." I swallow thickly at my screw-up.

Bren's lip quirks up at the side, and his chest heaves as though he's struggling to rein in his laughter.

Cal moves his head into the muffled conversation. "What happened?"

"I forgot Prince."

Cal seethes and then stares up at the ceiling before pinching the bridge of his nose. The guy looks like he's going to have a coronary, but I'm the kid's father, not him. I should be the one stressing. What the fuck is his problem? I shuffle uncomfortably on my feet before he responds with a nod of his head, as if he's pulled a plan together.

"Okay. You're the best man. Stay here, and I'll go and ask Sam to fetch him."

My shoulders sag in relief. I move back to my position

next to Con and avoid the tension and evil eyes radiating from Angel beside me.

A loud "ah" escapes the crowd, and I latch my eyes on Chloe, Cal and Lily's daughter. She's walking down the aisle, albeit reluctantly. She's now three years old and has one hell of a temper on her, so much so, we all hold our breath, hoping she will not react negatively.

How the hell Cal has kept it from Lily he tampered with her birth control for her to fall pregnant with Chloe is still a mystery. I'd have just told her we're having a kid. Deal with it.

Chloe's face like thunder proves she sure as shit isn't enjoying the limelight. I stifle a laugh at watching her get redder by the second, dragging her feet along the glass aisle as though purposely going slow.

Before long, the kid drops the basket of rose petals and kicks the damn thing down the aisle toward us. She crosses her arms over her chest and stands frozen on the spot.

Holy shit.

She glares up at Lily from under her long lashes. Lily's jaw tenses, and her cheeks redden in embarrassment. She glances around, no doubt looking for Cal. The guy is a Chloe whisperer; he's the only one who can calm the kid down when she starts with the tantrums. Pretty sure she's been watching Reece and throws one out there just to rival his.

And then, she drops on her ass, arms folded with a look of defiance.

Lily exhales and then storms down the aisle toward her.

Oh shit.

We all cringe at the fight now ensuing between them. Lily attempts to pick Chloe up, but the kid all out whacks her mom, her legs flaying in every direction like the goddamn kid from *The Exorcist*. "I want my daddy!" she screams.

The band plays louder to drone out her tantrum. I cast a glance toward Con to see how he's holding up. Having drama kick off before the service even starts is not ideal. Luckily, the dude is amused by the drama unfolding; his lips curl up in a smug grin he's trying to stifle.

Reece casually strolls down the aisle, bends, and whispers something into Chloe's ear, making the kid break out into a huge smile. She then takes Reece's hand and walks toward us with a skip in her step.

Lily, on the other hand, struggles to maintain a fake smile on her face. I choke on a laugh, which earns me a jab to my ribs by Angel.

Chapter Five

Con

The music changes once again, and my heart beats faster, pounding against my chest to the point of pain. My hands tremble slightly at the sight of my son walking slowly down the aisle toward me. His wavy brown hair is a mirror image of my own, his suspenders hold up his pants, and he has a small bow tie around his neck to match ours.

He pulls along a small wagon holding our dog Peppa and Reece's cat Pussy, both of which have bow ties on.

Keen smiles at me, and my heart soars at how amazing my little dude is; he holds his head high like I've been showing him, and I couldn't be any prouder. My shoulders broaden at the thought.

I bend down to greet him as he approaches, and my little man throws his arms around my neck. "Did I do good?"

I kiss his head and lift him. "So good, buddy."

"I have to go stand with Reece now, right?"

I pull back from our cuddle. "Yeah, dude. You got this." I drop him to his feet, and he fist bumps me before going and standing beside Reece.

I stand taller, watching the doors open at the end of the aisle.

The song "Fall Into Me" by Forest Blakk begins.

My heart hammers, and I swallow thickly with emotion when my gorgeous girl comes into view.

Jesus, she's breathtaking.

I choke, emotion clogging my throat, but I'm determined to not show it like a pussy.

I'm Mafia, for fuck's sake.

Will's hair is in soft waves framing her face, which is donning a genuine smile, and her green eyes hold mine with every step she takes. My heart beats faster. The chemistry radiates between us like we're the only people in the room. Her eyes hold me hostage, and I couldn't escape them even if I wanted to.

She looks stunning, with a fitted white dress that scallops around her tits. I bite my lip to ward off a moan.

Will's eyes flick up and down my body, taking in my tux. I don't miss the heat in her eyes, and I can't fucking wait to get on my knees for her and taste her in her wedding dress.

As my wife.

I place a delicate kiss on the side of her cheek, refraining from actually throwing her down here and now and reminding everyone who she belongs to.

Will takes hold of my hand. She draws lazy circles on mine with her thumb, as though silently asking me if I'm okay. I give her a firm nod, and she smiles at me, causing me to mirror her lips like a pair of loved-up teenagers.

Will

The officiant runs through the usual words, but all I see and hear is Con. I would never have imagined we'd ever get here. To marry my teenage love.

We've had so many trials and tribulations, it felt impossible.

But standing here today, opposite the man I love, the father of my son, is everything.

The officiant turns toward Con for him to say his vows.

Con doesn't pull out a piece of paper like I expect him to.

My eyes narrow with curiosity, and the grip he has on my hand tightens, pulling me in closer.

"Will, thank you for being here today. For standing by my side when I had nothing or no one. Thank you for being the one, the one who needed me as much as I needed you. I once thought it wasn't possible, that you'd never see me that way. But I know now, in here"—he touches his fist to his heart—"and here"—he points to his head—"there's only ever me for you, just like you for me. We need one another, love one another, and support one another. You not only gave me the best gift possible." His eyes catch on to our son, Keen, and I stifle a sob in my throat at the love pouring from my beautiful man. "You gave me life. You gave me hope, a future. Because without you both in it, I had nothing." He stares into my eyes pointedly. "Thank you for giving me you and for saving me from myself."

I blink back the tears and clear my throat. "Con, I've loved you all my life. Wanted you my entire life. Never in a million years did I think we'd be here today, declaring our love for one another. Thank you. Thank you for fighting for us." Con swallows hard, and his eyes fill with unshed tears. "Thank you for saving yourself." Con nods in understanding. "It's always been you." I stare into his eyes so he can see the truth seeping from mine. I need him to know although I married someone else, my heart always belonged to him.

Always.

He gives me a coy smile and breathes in deep, as though struggling to contain his feelings. "I love you, always."

"I love you so damn much, baby."

His lips crash to mine as applause breaks out around the room. My body feels like it's floating, floating on a cloud of love.

Floating with my man.

Chapter Six

Angel

I toe off my heels on a moan, kicking them beneath the table. I'm so fucking hungry right now, I could eat a damn horse.

I'm really hoping the speeches don't take too long.

Finn drops down beside me. "Just what the fuck's the problem?" He sneers in my direction, and I roll my eyes at his words.

I lazily turn my head in his direction, his blue eyes quickly analyzing my face, no doubt picking up on my pissy attitude. "You mean apart from forgetting our son?" I quip back at him.

He takes a toothpick out of his tux pocket and pops it in his mouth; he always does that when he's angsty. He nods. "Yeah, apart from that."

My jaw clenches at his nonchalance.

"Angel, he was fucking fine. He got to season four of

the pig show. Kid didn't give a shit. I mean, literally, no shit." He laughs awkwardly, knowing I'm not amused.

I sigh heavily and attempt to keep my voice low. "I'll tell you what the fuck my problem is, you ass . . ." His eyebrows rise at my tone, knowing I really am pissed. "You agreed we'd toilet train Prince before any more babies." His eyes narrow in confusion before he gives a firm nod in understanding. The dumb prick isn't getting it, not at all. I grit my teeth. "You knocked me the fuck up!"

His face morphs into shock before his lazy, cocky fucking grin returns. "Yeah?" His eyes are alight with joy.

Yeah? Is that all he has to say? Yeah? My chest rises and falls rapidly, anger bubbling to the surface.

I must look batshit crazy because Finn's face changes. He lowers his tone and moves toward my ear. "Darlin', that's amazing."

I glare at him, all out glare.

"What's the fucking problem?" he snaps again.

I move my head toward him so our faces are only an inch apart. "I'll tell you what the fuck my problem is. You didn't just put one baby in there. Two. Two fuckers, Finn."

Finn jolts at my words; his face pales slightly before he reverts back to his usual arrogant self. He shrugs and then throws me a sideways smirk. "Told ya, Darlin'. Monster cock, super sperm." He winks. Fucking winks. His chest puffs out like a goddamn moron, his body filling with pride, while all I want to do is rip his head off. My hand tightens on the glass of water the waiter just poured me. Fucking water . . . ugh.

Finn side-eyes me with a soft smile. "Darlin', it's only, what, seven fucking months to go?"

Only?

Then, I have to do the whole breastfeeding thing, colic, sleepless nights, and diapers. Oh my god. I can feel the panic bubbling inside me.

"Dad, Prince just stole my bread roll," Charlie whines from across the table, her face all scrunched up and on the brink of tears.

Finn snaps his eyes over to our son, who has now crawled onto the table like it's the most natural thing in the world. "Prince, give your sister her bread roll back."

Prince shakes his head at his father, and I can't help but inwardly smile at the shit about to go down. A nice pleasant reminder for Finn.

"Prince! Give her the roll." Finn's tone is darker; anyone else would back down, but not our son. Hell no, our boy is his father's double.

Absolutely no fear.

Prince stares back at Finn with a glare. His thick, dark, messy hair is a mirror image of his daddy's.

Once again, he shakes his head.

"Prince. The. Fucking. Roll. Give. Her!" Finn points and punctuates each word, deeper on each tone. The veins in his forehead protrude as he leans menacingly over the table. A stare-off commences between the two before Prince slowly moves the roll to his mouth. Charlie gasps at his audacity while I smile inside.

Finn launches across the table, causing Prince to quickly scurry back; he throws the roll across the table and kicks over the water jug while wrestling to get back in his chair.

Finn struggles to rein in his temper, knowing everyone will be watching; he bites his lip as he tries to shrug off the blatant lack of control he has over our toddler son.

I roll my head toward him and smile a sarcastic smile, saying just one word that sends the blood draining from Finn's face at the realization. "Two." I wink at him to add a little more injury to the insult.

Chapter Seven

Oscar

The ceremony went perfectly, executed as I fully intended. My eyes roam over the dining room, taking in the guests eating and mingling.

I notice Camille Varros acting odd; her eyes keep darting toward the door, as though she expects something to happen. But when I analyze her husband's body language, he's oblivious to her inner turmoil. Interesting.

I check my tablet once again. STORM Enterprises, along with our men, are taking the lead on security today. I feel as at ease as can be expected, given the circumstances.

Scanning the room again, I take in Dominik Kozlov. His eyes are firmly fixed on Anna Varros, the young daughter of Don Lorrenzo Varros.

Paige's soft hand strokes over my thigh, making me jolt to awareness. I stare down at my tablet, acting unperturbed by her simple touch, but my cock strains in my pants, causing me to forgo the speeches and instead give my woman pleasure. I push back in my chair and hold out my hand for Paige. Her green eyes flare with lust, making me wet my lips with my tongue. I tug her toward me as we leave the dining area.

I send Reece a quick message asking him to adjust the cameras accordingly.

"Where are we going?" Her heels click behind me as I make my way down the corridor and into the elevator.

As soon as the doors shut, I grip her throat and crash my lips to hers. Paige frantically works my belt, making me hiss in response when her soft palm encompasses my rock-hard cock.

I nip at her lip, the taste of blood fills my mouth, and my cock leaks with pleasure. I shove up her dress with one hand while the hand around her throat tightens, forcing her breathing to become labored. I close my eyes at the sensations of control and pleasure overwhelming me. She wraps her leg around my waist, giving me easier access to her bare pussy. It's dripping wet, allowing my cock to sink into her with ease.

"Mmm. Os," she moans into the kiss.

Slowly, I drift my lips down her neck, nipping and tugging at her bare flesh as my cock hammers into her silky warmth.

"I want to feel you come, Paige. I want to feel how much this pussy wants me."

She throws her head back, and her gorgeous red hair shimmers under the bright elevator lights.

Paige loves my filthy mouth, so I give in and let her

have it in droves. "A tight little pussy. All mine. I can feel your cunt milking my cock, begging to give you a baby."

"Oh my god. Yes. Yes, please."

"I want you swollen with my child, Paige."

"Please." She lets out a scream, forcing me to clamp down on her neck with my teeth to stop myself from groaning out loud. I pull her skin between my teeth as my cock floods her womb, determined to fill her with my child.

Paige sags against the elevator wall, her breathy pants causing a whisper against my ear.

"I love you, Oscar."

I turn my head to face her, our lips almost touching. "I know you do," I respond with a smirk.

Reece

Finally, the fucking speeches end, so we can enjoy our meals in peace.

Watching Chloe scrunch her nose at every item placed in front of her is comical; they specifically made the meals she likes, but she's less than impressed.

My dad has been trying to coax her for the past twenty minutes, but she's sitting with a face like thunder, refusing every damn thing, but then she suddenly perks up when they bring her ice cream.

I glance back down at my tablet, annoyance rumbling inside me.

When I so desperately want to tug on my hair to the point of pain, I do the breathing techniques Oscar has shown me—and uses himself—to control the rage bubbling inside me.

She promised me she wouldn't go out tonight, yet her apartment is glaringly empty; her tracker on her phone tells me she's left that behind, too. What the fuck?

I feel the hairs on my skin rise, and when I glance up, my dad's eyes drill into mine, making me narrow them quizzically. What the hell's his problem?

Chloe asks him a question, and his eyes dart away, but I don't miss the nervous bob of his Adam's apple. My hands tighten on the tablet with uncertainty.

"Everything okay?" My mom's soft, calming voice breaks me out of my thoughts.

I shuffle in my chair. "Everything's fine. Why wouldn't it be?" I snap.

"Just checking." She smiles back at me with sincerity, and I can't help but relax and smile back at her.

My mom calms me; she always has. But as I cast my eyes around the table once again, my dad's eyes are firmly on me again, making a sliver of unease fill my veins. His intensity, coupled with not being able to get in contact with her, makes me anxious, and when I get anxious, I lose control.

Not wanting to cause a disturbance, I push away from the table and decide to get some fresh air.

Chapter Eight

Will

Con's firm hand tightens in mine as he looks down on me with trepidation in his eyes. A flutter of nerves runs through me.

For months now, I've heard all about his elaborate plans for our wedding, and so far, I've been pleasantly surprised.

The ceremony and dining area are classy, with glass tables and crystal chandeliers that reflect the deep red of the roses beautifully; I can't believe he's created something so elegant, such a contrast to the zoo theme he'd originally planned.

I stare into his blue eyes as we stand in front of the large black drapes waiting to be pulled back to what I can only assume is the outdoor area. Con nibbles on his bottom lip, and I stifle a laugh at his nervous reaction. "What did you do?" I query with a raised eyebrow.

"Baby . . ." He licks his lips. "I just wanted everything."

I nod in understanding. Damn right he wanted everything. The whole family put a ban on hearing about any more of it.

I sigh. "Just pull back the drapes."

He gives a man in a suit a nod, and the drapes slowly pull back, revealing . . .

Holy shit.

Everyone gasps in shock? Delight? I'm not sure.

My eyes bug out.

"Mommy, it's a funfair!" Keen shrieks while making a run for the carousel.

I turn my attention back to Con as people push past to go outside. "You hired a funfair?"

He drags a hand through his hair. "Yeah."

My eyes flick over the grounds. The fairground lights illuminate the entire area, reflecting on to the lake. It looks amazing.

There are slides, a carousel, a helter-skelter, and a big wheel. There are traditional game stalls and fire breathers.

I turn back to Con. "I love it."

"Yeah?" A smile tugs at his lips, causing one to spread over my face.

"I really love it, Con." I nod reassuringly.

His lips crash down on mine, his tongue sweeping into my mouth as his hand tightens around my neck, holding me in place.

I'm aware of his hardness pressing into my hip. "Do I get a baby now?"

"Yes," I reply, draping my arms over his shoulders.

"Now?"

I glance around me; the dining room is now empty, as all the guests have left to explore the funfair.

"I stopped taking the pill," I admit in a whisper. His pupils dilate, and his nostrils flare; I can feel the sexual tension rolling off him.

"I need you." Before I can tell him he will have to wait, he's marching us toward the restroom.

It's empty as we enter. Con turns and locks the door, swallowing thickly when his eyes latch on to mine. He stands stoically still; his gaze roams over my body, taking in every inch and making my body light with a fiery need for him. There's a heat pooling between my legs, and a desperate need for him to touch me makes my breath stutter.

"You're my wife now, Will." His eyes darken. "If I want you to get on your knees and suck my cock, you'll do it." He stares at me, waiting for an argument, but I give him none. Instead, I relish in his words. "Like the good little Mafia wife, you'll do as you're fucking told."

We both know that's a lie. I'll fight him every step of the way and enrage him in the process, but we'll let him think it. For now.

I nod in agreement.

"I want to fuck you in your wedding dress. Then, I want you to leave here with my cum dripping out of your bare pussy with nothing between us, nothing stopping me from knocking you up."

I swallow thickly at his words because I want that too, more than anything.

"Can you lift your dress over your ass?"

I nod.

"Stand in front of the mirror and lift it."

I do as he asks.

He lowers himself to his knees.

My man. My husband. On his knees behind me.

A sharp smack hits my ass cheek, making me hiss. He snaps my white panties in two, letting them drop to the floor.

Con pushes me forward slightly, making me adjust my stance. He spreads my ass cheeks apart, and I moan as his warm tongue flicks over my tight asshole. "Oh god, Con."

"Mmm." He moans into my ass. His fingers move to my pussy, and he thrusts three fingers inside, making me wince at the sharp sting.

"Fuck yourself on my hand, Will."

I push back and forth against his fingers, loving the slurping noises behind me when his warm tongue laps over my hole. His grip tightens on my hip as I rock back and forth over his hand, forcing his fingers in and out of my slick pussy.

My walls clench around him. "Oh, Con."

Con withdraws his fingers, stands abruptly, and swipes his hand over his mouth. His reflection in the mirror above me is so intense, I can't help but whimper at the thought of what's to come.

His eyes roam down my bent body as he unbuckles his belt and pulls out his cock, the tip wet with pre-cum. "I nearly came in my pants, Will. What a fucking waste when I could be knocking you up."

I lick my lips and swallow hard, his eyes tracking every movement. "I'm going to fill this pussy up with so much cum, it'll have no option but to put a baby in you." The head of his cock is at my entrance. "I wonder if I can beat Oscar in knocking my woman up first," he muses, making me roll my eyes at his constant childish competitiveness.

Con snaps; he grips my neck and slams me down, pinning me hard against the counter, leaving my cheek flat so I can see him in the mirror.

I watch in awe as his mouth drops open, and with one hand on my neck and one on my hip, he hammers into me. "Oh, Con."

"Fuck, yeah. Scream my name while I fill you with my kid."

"More."

"Fuck. My dirty wife getting fucked in the restroom on her wedding day. Take my cock." He rams harder, making me wince at the aggression behind his actions. "Take all my cum."

I close my eyes at the intensity. The feeling of being controlled by him—used, and yet so devoted—makes my body putty in his hands.

"Open your fucking eyes. Open your eyes and watch me fill you with our baby."

My eyes snap open on command, locking with his in the mirror. Con's face is so tense, the veins on his forehead protrude with the strength behind each thrust. His hooded eyes watch me closely, causing my pussy to clench around him and sending me spiraling into my orgasm. "Yes. Yes. Yes."

"Oh fuck. Gonna fill you up."

Slam.

"Take it."

Slam.

"Take all my cum."

Slam.

He erupts inside me, so much that his cum flows out of my pussy and down my legs. Con sags against me, his heavy chest heaving up and down on my back. "Baby, fuck." He chuckles from behind.

"I know."

He raises his head to lock eyes with mine once again. "I love you."

"I love you too." I smile back with confidence.

Chapter Nine

Dominik Kozlov

I take another pull of my cigarette before blowing the smoke into the night air. The need to get away from here to relieve my aching tension, coupled with the need to touch her, is unbearable. It feels like my heart is in a fucking vise.

Not something I'm used to feeling.

Not at all.

Knowing she would be here today cemented my decision to accept the invitation. I'd also taken measures to make sure I could sit as close as possible without being too obvious of my intentions.

I have to bide my time. In what feels like a lifetime of waiting, I will soon have every piece in position to take what I want.

Her.

Taking another drag, I cast my eyes over the grounds; this has to be the most elaborate, ridiculous wedding I've been to in my entire life, and I'm Russian, so I've been to some pretty hyped-up weddings.

The younger O'Connell brother sure as hell meant what he said about making a statement.

A flash of her long golden hair catches my eye as she heads toward the tiger cage. I glance back in the direction she came from, expecting her bodyguard to follow her. But instead, there's a server who was practically drooling over her when he placed her meal in front of her. So much so, I bent the fork in my hand, causing the silver to cut into my meaty palm.

I hadn't felt a damn thing until my right-hand man, Dimitri, pointed out I was dripping blood onto the glass table.

The server scurries after her in the shadows, causing my spine to straighten with awareness. I push off the wall and follow behind, my body on alert at the sneaky shit's intentions.

I hang back around the corner of the cage, watching through the bars, listening in from a safe distance. My hand twitches to take out my knife and cut up the sly little prick who dared to follow her.

Anna is standing with her back to the fucker, so she doesn't see him approach. I watch his every move.

"Sooo, do you wann to have some ffun?" The punk's voice is slurred, like he's on something.

My hands curl around the bars, stopping me from going further and tearing him apart for even daring to speak to her. Part of me is desperate to remove him from the picture, yet another part is intrigued as to what the Mafia Princess thinks of this punk. Is this the kind of guy she's into? A sliver of jealousy racks through me. Yet again, another new emotion when it comes to her.

Her spine straightens at his words, but the prick misses her body language and pushes further. "I asked you a question, sweetheart."

She turns to face him, and the pain of seeing her turn toward him and not me makes my heart skip a beat, and my body trembles with a need to pull her into me. Force her to look at me, not him.

"Don't act all shy. I saw you checking me out."

She raises her chin and narrows her eyes in defiance.

That's my fucking girl.

"I was not checking you out." She scans his body in disgust. "You're a boy. I'm not looking for a boy. I need a man."

Hope blossoms inside me at her words. Damn fucking right she needs a man. She needs a man to protect her, care for her, and pleasure her. My cock aches in my pants, solid as a rock and wet with pre-cum.

His face screws up in anger. Slowly, he takes a menacing step toward her, but before he can step any farther, she holds out her palm to stop him.

The dumb fuck ignores her action, advancing on her with lust-filled eyes I recognize all too well, as each time I look at the photographs I have of her on my phone, my eyes fill with the same desire, consuming me to the point of physical pain.

I step out from beside the cage. Anna immediately

recognizes me, but instead of longing in her eyes, there's a glimmer of panic she quickly tries to mask.

Does she think I'm with this punk?

Does she think I will hurt her?

"Back off, man. She's mine. She's been playing hard to get all night," the punk snaps in my direction.

I'm six feet, five inches of solid muscle with tattoos covering all my body except my face. This kid can only be five feet, four inches and doesn't look as though he has a single muscle in his entire scrawny body.

"You with him?" I grunt out the words and nod my head in the punk's direction, never taking my eyes from her. This is the closest we've ever been, and my body knows it. Every cell in me comes alive, desperate for her to feel a spark, a glimmer of what I feel for her.

She bites her lip. "No."

Her soft voice makes my cock jump at the thought of her little pouty lips around it, sucking away. I stifle a groan and ignore the throbbing.

"Leave." I look to the kid, giving him the option to walk away that I wouldn't normally give. I don't want to scare her. I don't want her to see the monster inside me. My fists clench, struggling to maintain control.

I stare at the punk with such intensity there's no room for argument, but does the prick heed the warning? Of course he fucking doesn't.

Dumbshit.

He moves, but before he can pull what I can only assume is a weapon from his back, I have my knife out, flicked open and flying through the air straight into his shoulder. I follow through by rushing him into a choke-hold. I hold the little shit with ease, one of my thick arms banded around his neck, making it difficult for him to struggle.

"You might want to turn away, little one." My eyes lock on to hers, but rather than the expectancy of fear in her eyes, there's intrigue and, if I'm not mistaken, a little arousal, too. The thought makes my cock spurt in my pants.

I raise an eyebrow in question, giving her the option to turn and walk away.

"Do it." My body stills at her words. She's not what I expected. She's not the shy, meek wallflower I expected. No, she's strong and resilient; she'd be an asset, not a trophy wife Mafia men come to expect. And with that realization, it makes me want her all the more, as if that were ever possible.

I stare at her in question, and she stares right back at me with confidence, her shimmering blue eyes narrowing when I don't move to end the fucker.

"Anna?" She jolts at someone's voice in the distance.

Anna licks her lips. "My bodyguard," she explains without my prompting.

I give her a sharp nod, and without losing eye contact with her, I snap the prick's neck and drop him to the ground with a thud.

Anna turns to leave. Her silver dress shines under the lights, but it's her hair that my eyes latch on to. That golden, silky hair that makes my fingers twitch and my cock jump.

"I'll be seeing you soon, little one," I mumble into the night.

Real fucking soon.

I pull my phone and press call. "Get me a girl to play with. Blonde, the usual type." I hit end.

My hand strokes over my aching cock. "Soon, Anna. Real fucking soon."

Chapter Ten

Con

Keen runs ahead toward the tiger cage. I had to make huge donations to the Save the Tigers Foundation to get this thing here for him, so I'm pretty damn pleased he hasn't forgotten about asking for it like he did the roller-coaster that cost way more than Cal realized.

Turning the corner, I realize something is wrong because Keen stands frozen on the spot with wide eyes.

"Keen, buddy. What's wrong?" I flick my eyes back and forth between him and the pen.

"He's eating someone."

I chuckle at my kid. His imagination is like mine, full of crazy ideas coupled with a desperate need to create them, hence our elaborate wedding and multiple extensions on our mansion.

"Might want to get the lock fixed," a deep voice rumbles from behind, and I turn my head to face Kozlov.

The guy is a fucking psychopath, and that means something coming from me.

Glancing back at the pen, my eyes lock on to what I originally thought was meat, but now it's obvious it's a person.

I turn toward Kozlov in annoyance. If he's caused trouble at my wedding, I will flip the fuck out.

"A server kid, hassling the Varros Princess," he explains, as if hearing my thoughts, while taking a leisurely drag of his cigarette before turning and casually walking away.

"He has big teeth." My gaze snaps down toward Keen, almost forgetting my son is witnessing a man being brutally eaten. I expect to find terror in his eyes, but instead, my kid has a maniacal smile on his face as he stands with his hands on the bars of the cage.

My shoulders straighten as we stand side by side, watching the gruesome scene unfold before us.

Father and son.

The next generation of Mafia.

Chapter Eleven

Bren

I take hold of Sky's hand. "You remember when I won you those elephants at the boardwalk?" I turn to face her.

"Yes. Thank you, Bren."

I almost groan at her manners; her innocence hits me in the dick every damn time. My eyes roam over my girl. Fuck me, she takes my breath away.

The lights shining around us reflect off her long blonde hair; it blows in the wind, making her a vision.

I point over toward the stall just past the hotdog stand. It's the exact one from the night we spent at the boardwalk together.

Her eyes light up at the realization. "Bren, did you?"
"Yeah."

"That's amazing. Thank you." She stands on her tiptoes because, even though she wears heels, she's still so much shorter than me. Pressing a sweet kiss to her lips, I grip her ass and tug her toward me, forcing my tongue into her mouth aggressively. I grind my solid cock against her, causing her to whimper.

I allow her to pull back from me. "Can you win me a soft toy, please?"

"Sure." I smirk with confidence and stride toward the stall with her delicate hand in mine. "Which one?"

Sky nibbles on her lip, and her eyes dart around the stall, looking for the perfect soft toy. "The unicorn."

Our apartment is full of boy's shit, so a unicorn is a bit of a random request. "You sure?" I quirk a brow.

"Yes. When we have a daughter, she's going to be our little princess with all pretty girly things." She smiles at me innocently.

"Gotcha." Bending down, I kiss her forehead, then pick up the rifle, firing off the paintballs and hitting the target every time.

"Great. We're gonna be out of soft toys at this rate," the prick managing the stall grumbles as he unhooks the unicorn and hands it to Sky.

She smiles up at me as if I've given her the whole world, and truth be told, I would.

The lights around us change, and I know it's time to make our way over to the outdoor dance floor, the one I insisted was wooden to help replicate our whole night together at the boardwalk.

I lead her there; drawing her hand to my lips, I kiss her fingers tenderly. "Put your arms around me, baby." Sky looks up at me in confusion, but when I stare back down at her, she does as she's told and bands her arms around my waist, the damn unicorn stuffed between us.

The music changes, and as the beginning of our song "It's You" by Lewis Brice plays out, I relish the sound of her realization when she sucks in a sharp breath, and her eyes rise to meet mine. Hers shimmer with tears, but mine shimmer with pride.

Forever, I mouth to her.

"Forever." She smiles back.

Sam

"Sam!" Charlie runs toward me, and I open my arms to greet her. She rushes into me, knocking me back slightly with her excitement and making me chuckle at her enthusiasm. "Good to see you too, Princess." I kiss the top of her blonde head. The little girl is the spitting image of her mother, Angel.

When she draws back to smile up at me, a pang hits me in the chest; this kid gets me every time. I connect with her like no other, apart from the fact she clearly dotes on me, something I've never had before, and I can't help but love her hero-worshiping me, too.

Sure, I have people who fawn all over me, but this isn't the same; this is family. Charlie loves me, and I'd do anything for her and her family.

When I almost lost my life to help rescue Sky, the O'Connells could have discarded me, but instead, they paid for rehabilitation and therapy for my troubled past. They welcomed me into their homes, knowing my history with their uncle, but they trusted me, and in turn, I trusted them. So, when Cal asked if I'd help with security at Con's wedding, of course I was all in.

"Can you take me on the big wheel?" She grins up at me. Her forehead has a sheen of sweat from running around, and she rocks back and forth on the balls of her feet.

"Hey, babe." One of the two servers I fucked last night grazes her nails over my shirt while whispering into my ear, "Can you fuck us both again later?" My cock throbs at the thought of doing her and her friend again.

"Sam! I said can you take me on the big wheel?" Charlie's black eyes glare in the server's direction, her lip curled up in disgust.

I jolt, realizing I'm being come on to in the vicinity of a little girl. I clear my throat and step away from the server, ignoring her moans of contempt when I take Charlie's hand in mine and head toward the funfair.

Family comes first.

"You know, William Childs asked me out last week."

I open the door to the first cart, and Charlie gets in. I sit opposite her and wait for the ride to start. "What did you say?"

"I didn't say a damn thing; I kicked him in the balls for asking."

I choke on my spit.

"You have to know what you're good enough for, Sam. And William Childs is not good enough for me."

She raises her chin with a smug smile, and I can't help but break out into a grin. This kid is a force to be reckoned with. God help her parents when she becomes a teenager.

Charlie points toward the hotel as the wheel begins to slowly move. "That tramp back there tried to kiss my cousin Reece this morning." She spits the words out like vitriol. "Luckily, he has standards." She raises a questionable eyebrow in my direction, making me uncomfortable as hell that I'm getting a lecture about standards from a ten-year-old little girl.

I sigh and nod in agreement, unsure what the hell I'm supposed to say or do.

"Here, take this." She pulls something from the pocket of her cardigan and hands it to me, placing a small plastic ring down in the palm of my hand. "I won it on the lucky ducks. It's an engagement ring. When you meet the right girl, you can give it to her."

She stares at me genuinely, and I can't help but feel my chest tighten.

Not only are the wise words coming from a precious little girl, but without realizing it, Charlie has given me something I've never had before.

A gift.

My heart sinks at the realization that the first gift I've received is a plastic ring won on a lucky duck stall.

As if sensing my change in mood, Charlie folds my fingers over the ring. "It's special, Sam." My eyes become bleary at her words. "Just make sure she is, too."

She smiles at me as I repeat the words in my mind.

It's special, Sam. Just make sure she is, too.

Chapter Twelve

Will

Today has been everything and more; a feeling of completeness fills me. I take another sip of my champagne and smile to myself. This might be my last taste of alcohol for a while.

"Hey, Will. Congratulations." Jack approaches me with a genuine smile on his face. "I've already seen Keen running around here. He's keeping those nannies and guards on their toes." He laughs as he bends and kisses my cheek.

It's insane to think at one point, we were married; I look back now and wonder what we were thinking at the time.

We were lonely, I guess, and trying to create something to give us both a sense of security when, in reality, we were always going to be better off as friends.

He pulls back and looks me over, not a bit of arousal in them.

"You look cute."

I chuckle at his words, cute. Just what every girl dreams of hearing on her wedding day.

"Thank you." I smile back at him.

I see a shuffle of movement behind him, and Jack moves aside. My mouth almost drops open at the realization of the girl standing next to him, his stepsister, Lydia. "Lydia? Wow, you've grown!"

Lydia scoffs, earning a glare from Jack.

She feigns a smile. "Thanks." Then, she drops her smile and takes a drink from a bottle of water.

"I'm gonna go to the ladies room." She excuses herself and leaves Jack and me watching her walk away. When I told her she'd grown, I wasn't kidding. The last time I saw her, she was a teenager. Now, she looks anything but.

"What, er . . ." I point my champagne glass in Lydia's direction.

"What's her deal?" Jack scrubs a hand over his cropped hair. "She's a pain in my ass, that's what. My father's gone away on business, and I'm left to deal with that." He points his beer bottle in her direction.

"Hey, baby." Con's hand wraps around my waist, tugging me backward toward him, away from Jack. He kisses my neck and tightens his hand on my waist, clearly pissing on his territory. I roll my eyes at his jealous antics.

Jack doesn't miss a single movement, and I can tell he's struggling to stifle a laugh. No matter how many times I reassure Con that Jack and I are just friends, he still becomes jealous whenever I'm in his presence.

"Your date is flirting with the security." Con points

over Jack's shoulder toward Lydia, making my eyes bug out at her clear display of interest in the security guy, although he seems quite taken with her, too.

Jack turns, his shoulders straighten, his nostrils flare in rage, and his jaw tics. Yeah, the guy is pissed.

"Thanks for having me, guys. I'll speak to you both later," he mumbles the words as he storms in Lydia's direction without so much as giving us a backward glance.

"You did that on purpose."

Con chuckles in my ear. "Maybe."

"You do realize you just got his little sister in trouble." I spin in his arms to face him.

He shrugs. "I thought she was his woman. Anyway, forget about that douche."

I'm about to open my mouth and tell him not to call Jack that, but he cuts me off.

"Come see. I have a surprise for you."

I take a deep breath, unsure I can take any more surprises.

Cal

I lean against the balcony railing, taking in the scene before me.

I'll give Con his due; the funfair worked out spectacularly. The guests are in awe, and everyone is having a great time.

I can relax knowing that Finn's ex-serviceman buddy who co-owns STORM Enterprises is helping control security tonight.

I glance down at my watch once again, knowing the plan I put in place before coming here is now well underway.

Soft hands wrap around my chest, and I instantly recognize them as belonging to my wife, Lily. She nuzzles into my neck. "You seem really wound up tight." Her soft lips trail around my open collar, and her hands stroke over the top of my shirt and down my abs, stopping at my waistband.

My heart rate escalates, and my cock pulsates. "Are

you going to fix it?" I query nonchalantly, taking another swig of my drink.

"I am."

I turn to face her, leaning back on the railing with my arms stretched on either side and my legs parted. I take in my stunning wife. Her gorgeous brunette locks are in soft waves down her back, and loose strands blow in the breeze around her face.

My heart hammers faster at the sexual chemistry between us.

Lily slowly kneels to the ground, her eyes locked on mine.

My hand tightens on my glass while the other grips the railing to stop myself from reaching out and shoving her face into my crotch.

She painstakingly slowly drags my zipper down. Her hand works to open my belt, and I hiss through my teeth when her soft palm connects with my cock. I close my eyes at the sensation of her warm breath whispering over the dripping head.

"Lily," I warn when she makes no move to connect her mouth with my cock. She smirks in response, annoying the hell out of me. "Just fucking suck it before I face-fuck you in your pretty dress."

That gets her moving. My head falls back on a groan when her wet tongue grazes over my cock from bottom to top and back again. "The tip, baby. Play with the tip."

Lily braces one hand on my thigh, and the other plays with my balls, stroking them and tugging them. My whole body alights at her touch.

When her tongue dips into the slit of my cock to swipe away the pre-cum, I swear it takes everything in me to not fuck her face.

Her mouth covers my cock and bobs up and down, and strings of her saliva mixed with my pre-cum drip onto my balls.

"Fuck."

I drone out the noise from below us; the laughter and chaos no longer exist. It's just the two of us.

My gorgeous wife on her knees before me, worshiping my cock.

"Mmm, more, baby."

She slurps, her moans vibrating around my cock, causing the familiar tingle to gather in my balls.

I grit my teeth and glance down to watch her. Her eyes are locked firmly on mine. "Swallow every bit."

She blinks in response and works her hand over the base of my cock. My hips work without instruction, pushing further into her.

"Fuck, it's coming. Fucking take it all." My mouth drops open on a grunt as my cum floods into her mouth, filling it with my essence. "So fucking beautiful."

Her green eyes sparkle back at me with desire.

"Ladies and gentlemen, we'd like you to gather by the lake for the grand finale." The speaker makes us jolt, breaking us out of the moment.

I exhale in disappointment and hold my hand out for Lily, who takes it after she tucks my spent cock into my pants, saying, "Don't worry, your ma is having Chloe tonight."

I laugh at her words and draw her in for a quick kiss.

"I think Ma is having all the kids tonight."

Lily smiles back at me. "I think you're right."

I guess all my brothers are taking advantage of Ma's babysitting skills and keeping her busy following our da's recent departure.

"Come on, we best go and see what he's got planned now." Lily rolls her eyes in jest, making me snort in laughter.

I must admit, Con has done an amazing job. I just hope we make it through the night with no drama.

Chapter Thirteen

Con

We stand by the edge of the lake with the lights from the funfair reflecting on to the water with the mountains surrounding us. I feel a sense of calm wash over me.

She's mine now, as she always should have been.

With her hand entwined in one of mine and our son, Keen, in my other, we stare out at the water.

"Daddy, what's going to happen?"

"Just wait and see." I kneel beside Keen, taking in my little dude's features, the familiar pang of guilt hitting me at not being there for the first few years of his life—along with the panic I feel when I consider I might never have had him in my life—hits me hard in the chest, making me suck in sharply, gasping for air.

Will's hand trails down my spine, leaving behind a wake of goose bumps. "I love you," she reassures me as always.

I turn to face her; her hazel eyes latch on to my own. "I love you too, baby."

The lights go out, and everyone around us gasps, not knowing what's about to happen.

Like clockwork, lights glow on the mountains, creating a perfect scripture of "Con and Will."

Music begins and "Nobody Knows" by The Lumineers comes through the speakers.

I stand and pull my wife and son into me; the floats on the water light up one by one, creating a display of the word, "Always," along with hearts surrounding the word in the distance.

"It's beautiful." Will squeezes me tighter.

I kiss her hair. "I love you, baby."

"I love you too."

Fireworks explode into the sky, and the booms vibrate through our bodies.

Gasps and hollers encircle us as we embrace the finale of the night.

"I can't wait to see where our future will take us, Con."

I stare down at my wife, my lips curling into a grin at the thought of my new endearment. "Me too, baby. Me too."

Finn

"Your ma has the kids, right?" Angel scurries after me as I stride into the clearing in the forest.

"Yeah, Darlin', chillax. Kids are fine." I wave my hand toward the funfair, knowing if Ma doesn't have the kids, I'm sure a nanny or one of the guards will. There's no doubt in my mind that the kids are safe.

I can hear the music playing in the distance, and I know the fireworks will go off soon. I also know my cock will be irritated soon if I don't stick myself in my woman any second. I've waited all damn day to take her.

I even planned the perfect spot, and I timed it just right.

"Are we there yet? My feet are killing me!"

I turn and face the water; the rock in front of me is the perfect spot for Angel to cling on to as I fuck her from behind.

"Here." I point toward the rock.

Angel draws back and pulls a face as though not impressed with my grand gesture.

"Here?" She turns her nose up.

"Yeah, Darlin'. Here."

Stepping forward, I pull her into me and kiss those pouty lips before she even protests. When she melts into me, I know I have her. My hand tangles in her hair as hers fumble to unbuckle my belt.

"Oh god, Finn."

"Fuck, Darlin'. Really want to fuck your ass. You gonna let me?" She doesn't answer me; instead, she moans into my mouth, and I take that as a yes.

I pull away and spin her to face the rock.

"Open the zipper, Finn!" she snaps over her shoulder.

Jesus fucking Christ, my cock is rock hard, and she wants to waste time getting her naked.

My hand trembles with anticipation as I struggle to slide the zipper down her delectable body.

The dress pools at her feet, and she moves aside to pick it up and drape it over a branch.

Angel moves back into position and wiggles her bare ass at me. Her thighs have sexy lacy red garters with ribbons around them, and her heels are bright red to match them.

I pull my leaking cock out of my boxers. "Fucking Jesus, Angel. No panties?" My words come out stuttered as I struggle to rein in my need for her. Pre-cum flows from the tip.

Giving it a rough stroke with my palm, my eyes fill

with lust as they trail down Angel's spine and down the crack of her ass, stopping on her asshole. Her wet pussy is glistening in the nightlight.

"Fuck, Darlin'. You look so damn hot."

She raises her head, looking over her shoulder, and says, "Shut up and spank me for being dirty."

I shuffle closer to her, wrap my hand around her white-blonde hair, and tug it back sharply. "Don't fucking tell me what to do, Angel!" *Smack.* My palm stings at the impact, and my cock jumps, wanting in on the action. "Rub your pussy, Darlin'," I grit out with bare restraint.

Angel begins to frantically move; I stand behind her, watching the motion of her fucking herself over her hand.

I push two fingers into her pussy, making her jolt and moan at the intrusion. Gathering her pussy juice, I withdraw and stroke it over her ass before bending my neck and spitting onto her hole for more lubrication.

"Can't believe I've knocked you up, Darlin'."

"I know."

"You happy?" I drag my cock up and down over her ass, waiting for the perfect moment to push inside. "Darlin'?" I question again.

"Yes."

"Good girl."

The rumble of fireworks begins, and I ram my cock into her so goddamn hard, we slam into the rock, shocking myself with the impact.

"Fuck, Darlin', you okay?"

"Yes. More."

I draw back onto my feet and take her hip in one

hand and her hair in another. Tugging her head back so she can see over the lake, I slide in and out of her perfect ass at a slow pace.

The ground vibrates with the pressure of the explosions, and that's my cue to move faster.

"Oh god, Finn!"

"Fuck yeah." My hips hit her ass cheeks as I pound into her repeatedly. She clenches around me, my balls tingling when her warm muscles contract.

"Harder."

I slam into her with aggression behind my movement, and my teeth grit together to ward off my impending orgasm.

The fireworks light us up, the booming noise around us almost deafening. I've never seen such a beautiful sight, balls deep in the woman I love.

My wife.

"Finnnn." Angel clenches around me, her muscles so tight, I can't hold back any longer.

"Fuck. Fuck. Fuck." I come so hard, I see stars. Only when my cock is milked dry do I open my eyes to the reoccurring realization.

There's nowhere else I'd rather be.

Chapter Fourteen

Oscar

I stare down at Paige. She's tied to the bedposts with the ropes I brought along specifically for this trip.

Her milky skin is perfect, shining beautifully from the lights seeping in from the open balcony doors.

I slap the flogger against the palm of my hand, and the action makes Paige attempt to clench her thighs. Of course, she's incapable of doing so while her ankles are tied to the posts.

My cock jumps at the thought of her being immobilized, completely at my submission, to use and abuse her body as I see fit.

Her nipples are redder than normal, and not for the first time, I wonder if she's pregnant. I won't allow myself the privilege of checking her hCG levels. I'm enjoying the thoughts of getting her pregnant far too much; the determination to breed her has consumed me.

Paige now has a structured diet, takes fertility-enhancing drugs, and we have sex multiple times a day when her cycle app informs me of the perfect opportunity to impregnate her.

"Are your nipples painful?"

Her cheeks flush at my blunt words. "A little."

"Do you want me to suck them into my mouth?"

"Oh god, Os." She attempts to wiggle to no doubt take the edge off her needy pussy.

"Mm. I think you want me to suck them into my mouth then mark them with my cum, don't you, Paige?"

Her chest heaves up and down on a moan, "Yes."

"Mmm. But we both know that's not going to happen, don't we?"

She swallows thickly. "Yes."

I stare down at her beauty, her perfect skin unmarked, ready for me to claim.

"Why?" I raise an eyebrow while I wait for her to repeat the words I tell her.

"Because you want me pregnant, and until then, all your cum is going to be used to fill my pussy."

"That's right, so you need to be a good girl and be patient. When you're full with my child, then I'll allow you to wear my cum. Understand?"

"Yes."

I suck in a sharp breath, unable to hold back any longer. I raise the flogger and bring it down on her pussy with a slap. She raises her ass off the bed. "Oh god."

Slap.

"More."

Again and again, I slap her pussy, watching it glisten with her juices.

"We're going to get married."

Paige lifts her head, and her eyes widen.

"Say yes," I demand as I stare down at her with such intensity, it leaves her with no other option than to agree.

Her voice comes out weak. "Yes."

I nod at her words, satisfied that she did as asked. And now, I can reward her with my cum.

I drop the flogger and position myself between her legs. Knowing her cunt is dripping for my cock, I ram into her, making her arch her back at the intrusion, and her mouth drops open on a whimper.

"You feel so good around my cock, Paige. Fucking you bare." I thrust into her harder before pulling most the way out and ramming into her again.

With one hand around her neck, I tighten my grip, pressing on her pulse point. Paige's eyes flare in both panic and arousal, and her chest heaves up and down, bringing attention to her perfect tits.

She struggles to speak before mumbling, "Please." But it's labored.

"You want me to suck your tits?" She blinks her eyes in confirmation. "Dirty fucking girl, always wanting more." I dip my head to her nipple and lick over the peak; her pulse races under my touch, making my balls draw up with the knowledge she wants me as much as I want her.

"Mmm." She moans when my mouth gently suckles around her nipple. "Oh, Os." I grind my hips against her, making her pussy muscles contract around me. "I want your cum."

Fuck. I love it when she asks for it.

"Please, Os. Give it to me."

I love it when she begs.

"Oh, fuck." I pull back and thrust into her with such force, the bed hits the wall again and again until her pussy tightens around my cock like a vise.

"Yes! I'm—" Her mouth drops open on a scream, loud enough to drone out the noise coming from the open doors leading to outside.

Her climax triggers my own; rope after rope of cum floods her womb. I continue to move inside her until my balls are drained and my cock is spent, finally allowing myself to fall on top of her, my face nestled against her tits.

"I love you, Os."

I kiss her breast tenderly. "I know." I smile back, plucking her flesh into my mouth to leave a mark.

Closing my eyes, I will my seed to take.

To leave an everlasting mark on us both.

"I love you too."

Reece

I lift my Pussy from out of the basket, feeling the need to carry her with me. I make my way out the patio doors, and I come to a halt when I see Camille, who has recently married Luca Varros, her family's sworn enemy.

She looks hot as hell in her tight dress and high heels but not as hot as my woman. Clearly, I have a thing for older women. When I finally made that realization a couple of days ago, I didn't get to act on it. But as soon as we're home from this trip, I will rectify that problem. Yes, it will all change.

I hadn't intended on becoming embroiled in a love triangle, especially one with an older woman. But I'm man enough to accept I was wrong; I just need to prove it to her.

I nuzzle my face into Pussy when a ripple of anxiety flows through me.

She's pissed and ignoring me. I'll let her have these

couple of days, but when I get home, I won't stand for this shit any longer.

We were destined to be together, so it's time I show her.

I watch as Camille Varros hides in the shadows against the wall while everyone is watching the firework display, and I wonder where she's going or who she's trying to escape from. Glancing up at the camera above her, I shake my head at her naivety; the silly girl is going to get herself in trouble.

"Hey, kid." I turn to the cold voice behind me. Taking in Luca, I notice his ruffled hair, and I can see the tic in his jaw that he's trying to disguise. His chest rises fast, as though he's been rushing. His black eyes bore into mine as though trying to intimidate me. "Have you seen my wife anywhere?"

I take a moment to decide on my next course of action before sighing in boredom. I decide to act dumb because I sure as shit do not look like a kid, yet this jackass thought he could insult me by calling me one.

"I don't know who you are." I give him a careless shrug, all the while willing Camille Varros the best of luck in whatever she's planning on doing.

His eyes narrow on me, as though trying to gauge whether I'm being serious or not. I smirk slightly at the thought, but the dick clearly isn't as dumb as I originally thought because he catches the smirk.

"I'm Luca Varros, but I think you know that already. Don't you?" He steps toward me, his eyes drilling into mine. With his slicked-back dark hair and broad shoulders, he stands out a mile as an Italian key player in the Mafia, but I'm not about to let him in on the secret as to where his wife is.

Giving her a little more time in no doubt her bid for freedom, I invite him to pet my best friend. "Would you like to stroke my Pussy?" He startles, and his eyes bug out at my words, so I hold my cat up toward him, causing a disgusted grimace to break out on his face. He surveys me up and down, as though checking to see if I have all my limbs and no doubt searching for a problem with me. "Pussy likes being stroked."

A guy I recognize as one of the guards rushes into the room, clearly out of breath. "Boss. I checked the restrooms. She isn't there."

Luca's spine straightens, and his shoulders tighten. He gives me one last look over before deciding I know nothing, and he turns without another word or backward glance.

"Check the security footage," he snaps at his guard.

"We'd better wipe that footage, Puss," I tell my cat as I place her on the dining table and take out my phone to locate all footage of Camille over the past hour.

That should give her a head start and teach that fuck face a lesson, too.

Rule one, never judge a book by its cover.

Rule two, don't call me a kid. I'm very much a man.

A Mafia man.

Chapter Fifteen

Lily

I flop down on the couch beside Angel. Her feet are bare and covered in dirt, making me wonder what she's been up to.

"Don't ask." She smirks at me, her blue eyes alight with happiness.

I stifle a giggle at her response, realizing she probably just had sex with Finn outside somewhere. Hopefully away from view.

"Where have they all gone?" Paige asks from opposite me. Since joining the O'Connell family, she's fit right in, and I love her like a sister.

I know she harbors guilt about what occurred the night she was kidnapped, but things happen for a reason, and those things brought her and Oscar together. She gave my brother-in-law something nobody else could give. Hope. A future. Happiness. And for that, I'll be eternally grateful.

Paige sees past Oscar's differences and into the man himself. A man who would do anything to protect his family, protect those he loves the most. She loves him for him, despite his differences.

I can only hope that my son, Reece, finds someone like her. Someone who loves him for him, the fiercely loyal and loveable man he's become.

"They've gone down to the lake." I smile back at Paige, and she gives me a nod, understanding that the guys have gone to no doubt discuss how the day has gone. Having so many Mafia families under one roof has been stressing Cal out for months now, so I, for one, am happy it will be over.

Will approaches, still looking incredible in her wedding dress, despite the just-fucked look she's rocking. "You looked pissed at Finn earlier." She quirks a brow at Angel while dropping onto the couch.

Angel scoffs. "Yep." She pops the p. "Pissed is an understatement."

I shuffle to face her. "What happened?"

Angel exhales dramatically. "I'm pregnant."

All the girls congratulate her, and she feigns a smile.

"You're not happy?" I take her hand in mine, knowing myself that finding yourself pregnant when you least expected it can leave you with many emotions, guilt being a hard one to contend with.

"I am . . ." She drops back into the cushions. "Prince is such a handful, and Charlie is just . . ." She waves her hand around the room, making us all nod in agreement.

Charlie is most definitely dramatic, sassy, and determined.

She sighs loudly. "And I'm having twins." My eyes bug out.

"Twins?" I repeat.

The girls all suck in air, now understanding Angel's concerns.

Sky claps her hands together, and her long blonde hair touches her knees as she leans forward. A large smile encompasses her face. "How wonderful. I've always wanted twins."

Angel's glare toward her looks murderous.

"I hope I'm having twins, too. Can you imagine?" She places a hand on her stomach with a loving, faraway gaze.

"Oh my gosh, Sky. Are you pregnant, too?" Will chimes in as we all look at one another in shock at the latest bombshell.

Sky jolts slightly, as though being brought out of her daydream. "I think so. Bren has been trying very hard to breed me."

"Breed you?" Angel's voice oozes disgust.

"Sounds like something I hear in the clinic." Paige coughs, smothering a laugh. Then, she bites her lip, as if trying to stop herself from saying more.

"He's so growly, too." Sky smiles to herself. The girl sure looks like she's the cat that got the cream and is not the least bit perturbed by the fact her husband refers to breeding her—like an animal.

"Does he put a collar on you too?" Will asks her jokingly.

But when silence fills the room, and Sky's face looks somewhat stunned, we all sit and wait for a response, because now I'm intrigued.

Her hand flies up to her neck. "No, he doesn't. Should I ask him to?" She looks around us all quizzingly, as though we're about to tell her that her husband should collar her while he breeds her. The thought makes a laugh bubble up inside me at her naivety in every conversation we have.

It's then I take note of Paige. Her face has gone beet red, making it obvious she's hiding something.

"Holy shit. Oscar collars you?" Angel leans forward on the couch with intrigue.

Paige's green eyes dart around us. "Sometimes." She shrugs.

"I bet he's all growly, too." Angel grins in delight, clearly enjoying the topic of conversation.

"He can be demanding." Paige looks down at her clasped hands, and it's only then my eyes latch on to a ring on her finger that most definitely wasn't there this morning.

"Paige? Are you engaged?"

Her eyes dart up to mine, and she nibbles her lip. "Apparently so."

I choke on her words while they sink in. *Apparently so.*

These O'Connell men sure know how to take what they want, questions be damned.

Will stands up first, followed by Sky, Angel, then

Paige. I follow the girls as we all pull together for one big hug.

"O'Connell sisters rule!" Angel hollers.

"Hell yeah!"

"Mom!" Reece shouts from behind us with urgency in his voice, making us all pull quickly apart. "We got a problem . . ."

Chapter Sixteen

Con

Today has been the best day of my entire life.

I stand at the water's edge to reflect on our wedding day while Will tucks Keen into bed in Ma's room. Staring out over the lake, I can still hear guests still enjoying themselves, the music from the band, and the sound of the funfair in the distance.

"Hey, you good?" Finn approaches with a cigarette hanging from his mouth.

"I thought you stopped smoking?" I look him up and down like he's crazy because Angel will go mad if she smells smoke on him.

"I did." He drags a hand over his already messy hair.

"Been a good day, brother." Bren walks down the slope toward the water.

"Yeah, it has." I grin to myself. "It's been fucking epic."

"The carousel was a hit with the kids." Cal muses as

he kicks dirt from under his shoes, then bends down to pick up a rock before skimming it out over the water. "Wait, are you smoking?" Cal turns toward Finn with a look of disgust on his face.

"Fucking Jesus. I'm smoking; get the fuck over it."

"Why?" I can't help but ask because Finn looks close to freaking out, so something has tipped him over the edge. It must be bad if he's risking his balls being cut off for a quick drag.

"Angel's knocked up."

Bren breaks out into a huge-ass grin while I feel a sliver of jealousy course through me before quickly kicking that to the side.

Cal's eyebrows furrow in confusion. "That's good news, right? You've been wanting another baby."

"Yeah. She's having twins." He sighs heavily while we all hang on his every word.

Twins? Jesus.

"Prince just shit on the bathroom floor, and Charlie slipped in it; she's a goddamn drama queen." He rolls his eyes. "Damn stuff will wash out of her hair, and I'll buy her a new bridesmaid dress." He shrugs as though it's nothing, but obviously, it's turned into drama for him to be out here puffing away. "Angel's blaming me for it all."

"You did tell her you'd toilet train Prince before you knocked her up," Oscar offers as he steps out from behind the tree line.

Finn grins and grabs his crotch. "Super fucking sperm."

We roll our eyes and moan at his dumb words, but

truth be told, I hope to God my swimmers work as good as his. I can't wait for Will to have my baby. For me to experience everything I missed with Keen. I ignore the pain in my chest and push away the feelings of guilt.

"I'm marrying Paige," Oscar throws out nonchalantly.

"You ask her?" Bren raises an eyebrow in question.

Oscar scoffs and picks invisible lint off his shirt. "I told her." His dark eyes glare into Bren's. Of course he told her. It's what us O'Connells do. We see what we want, and we take it. I grin from ear to ear at the thought of our family expanding. The future generations of O'Connells.

The rumble of motorcycles makes all our heads turn toward the entrance to the resort, my eyes widen in realization, and I turn to Oscar. "Teddy came?"

"Bit fucking late," Finn snipes the words out, sounding like a petulant child.

"Finn, make him feel welcome." Cal glares in my brother's direction.

Bren stands taller, as though ready for battle. "That's a fucking order."

Finn nods in agreement before lighting another cigarette.

Oscar stares down at his phone. "It appears he brought some of his club brothers with him."

"Fan-fucking-tastic. It's turned into a goddamn circus after all," I grumble, knowing the tone has now been lowered by having a bunch of bikers at my wedding.

"You're such a pussy," Finn quips.

"Did someone say pussy?" Reece strolls along the water's edge toward us, kicking stones into the water as he lazily drags his feet.

"Yeah, Finn won't be eating any for a while because he's started smoking again." Bren chuckles.

"Pregnant women have an amazing sense of smell," Cal agrees. "I read about it when Lily was expecting Chloe."

"Of course you fucking did." Finn rolls his eyes.

"I came to tell you guys we have a problem." Reece drags a hand over his hair in agitation, but before his words come out, two men run toward us. Bren draws his gun on instinct from behind his back.

As they approach, I recognize one as Luca Varros and the other as his guard. "My wife is missing, and the security footage is gone. I want this place locked down. Right fucking now!"

I turn to Oscar, who is already tapping away on his phone, and Bren, who is now barking orders into his phone.

"We'll sort it. Head up toward the reception, and we'll meet you there; she can't have gotten far," Cal calmly tells them both. Luca looks like he's about to argue, but after casting his eyes around my brothers and realizing they're working to help him, not hide her, he nods at his guard, and they both turn toward the hotel.

"I think we need to get everyone inside," Reece suggests, shifting from foot to foot.

"To do a headcount? Might be easier that way to find her, I mean," Cal suggests.

"Nope. I mean, with the tiger being out."

My blood runs cold on his words. We all stop what we're doing and turn toward Reece.

He glares back at us all. "I didn't fucking do it! Don't look at me!"

"The tiger's out?" Cal repeats like an idiot.

Reece nods. "Yeah."

"Holy. Fucking. Shit." My heart races; thank fuck the kids are inside now with Ma.

Bren turns toward me, his eyes alight with rage; before I know what's coming, I feel the force of his fist against my jaw. "A fucking tiger! You dumbass. Who the fuck has a tiger at their wedding?"

I grind my jaw from side to side, making sure it still works. "At least it'll be memorable." I try to lighten the mood.

Bren, Oscar, and Cal ignore my quip and work frantically on their phones while racing toward the hotel.

Finn turns to me and huffs out a puff of smoke.

"Best wedding ever, brother." He puts his fist out for me to bump, making me break out into a cocky smile.

Damn fucking right best wedding ever.

THE END

Acknowledgments

I decided not to write a huge acknowledgment list this time, as the list would probably be longer than the book.
A huge thank you to TL Swan for giving me the opportunity to join her amazing writing group. Without her not a single book would exist.
And to each and every one of you that has supported me through the Secret And Lies Series.
Your support is appreciated.
I love these guys so much.
Be sure to look out for them in future books, along with the short stories based on each character.
Thank you from the bottom of my heart.
BJ Alpha

Also by BJ Alpha

Secrets and Lies Series

CAL Book 1

CON Book 2

FINN Book 3

BREN Book 4

OSCAR Book 5

SECRETS AND LIES SHORT STORIES

CAL

CON

FINN

BREN

OSCAR

Born Series

Born Reckless

The Brutal Duet

Hidden In Brutal Devotion

Love In Brutal Devotion

The Brutal Duet Part Two

About the Author

BJ Alpha lives in the UK with her hubby, two teenage sons and three fur babies.
She loves to write and read about hot, alpha males and feisty females.

Follow BJ on her social media pages:
Facebook: BJ Alpha
My readers group: BJ's Reckless Readers
Instagram: BJ Alpha

And don't forget to sign up to BJ's Newsletter for exclusive information and competitions. Newsletter sign up.

Printed in Great Britain
by Amazon